WALT DISNEY PRODUCTIONS'

the Fox and the Hound

Golden Press • New York
Western Publishing Company, Inc.
Racine, Wisconsin

Big Mama the owl looked down from her perch high in a tree. Something was lying in the tall grass. A small, furry something that hadn't been there before. The old owl was puzzled. What could it be?

Big Mama had to know everything. So she spread her wings and glided down for a closer look.

"Fuss my feathers!" she gasped. "A baby fox! Some hunters must have chased his mother — and now he's alone in the world."

The little fox looked up at Big Mama with sad eyes.

"Don't you worry, darlin';" Big Mama said softly.
"Everything will be all right. We'll find someone to take
care of you."

Dinky the sparrow and Boomer the woodpecker came
fluttering over to see what Big Mama was doing. "What
a cute little fox," they said. "But he needs a home."

The birds decided that Widow Tweed, a kindly old
woman who lived nearby, would take good care of the
baby fox.

"How can we get her to find him?" asked Boomer.

"I have a plan!" Dinky chirped.

Dinky and Boomer snatched some laundry from the widow's clothesline.

"Come back with my wash!" cried Widow Tweed, chasing them. "Come back here, you silly birds!"

The birds flew right to the spot where the baby fox was hidden and dropped the laundry on top of him.

Widow Tweed came huffing and puffing after them. When she picked up her laundry, she found a surprise.

"A dear little fox!" she exclaimed. "And no mother to look after you? Why, that will never do!"

She took the fox back to her farmhouse. "I'm going to call you Tod," she said. "I'll take good care of you. And you'll be good company for me."

In her cozy kitchen, Widow Tweed held Tod in her lap and fed him milk from a bottle.

Big Mama, Dinky, and Boomer watched happily from the window. They knew that their baby fox had a good home.

That same day a hound-dog puppy also found a home, in a cabin near the widow's farm. The cabin belonged to a rough, grumpy hunter named Amos Slade.

Amos chugged up to his cabin in his pickup truck. He took the pup out of the truck and set him down in front of Chief, his old hunting dog.

"Look here, Chief," he said. "This pup's name is Copper. Take good care of him. I'm going to teach him to be a real smart hunter, like you."

Old Chief wasn't sure he *wanted* another hound around the place. But Copper was cute and friendly, so Chief decided to make the best of it.

Tod and Copper both liked their new homes. Tod spent his days happily in Widow Tweed's barnyard. And Copper played near Amos's cabin while Chief dozed in the sun.

One day the little fox was chasing a butterfly. Over a stone wall he went, through a field of wildflowers, and into a patch of woods near Amos's cabin.

Copper was playing in Amos's yard as usual. Suddenly he stopped. His nose began to twitch.

"What's that interesting new smell?" he asked Chief.

"Nothing," Chief said drowsily. "The master's just cooking."

But Copper knew it wasn't a cooking smell. He wanted to find out more. So he followed his nose out of the yard and into the woods. Suddenly he bumped into Tod.

The fox and the hound stared at each other. Tod wiggled his ears. Copper wagged his tail. Tod gave a questioning yip. Copper replied with a friendly little bark. Before long they were playing hide-and-seek.

Tod and Copper had so much fun that they played together every day after that. All summer they romped through the woods and across the sunny meadows.

Big Mama, Dinky, and Boomer watched the young playmates.

"Gracious me!" said Big Mama. "It's *very* unusual for a fox and a hound to be so friendly. It just isn't done! But they do like each other. Let's hope for the best."

One day when Tod came to Amos's to get
Copper, he found his friend tied in the yard.

"The master says I have to stay home,"
Copper said sadly.

"That's okay," said Tod. "There's lots to do
here." He looked into Chief's barrel. The old dog
was dozing there.

"Tod, don't!" Copper warned as Tod crept into
the barrel. But it was too late. Chief was awake.
He growled angrily.

Tod ran. Chief bounded after him, the barrel
crashing and clattering through the yard. Amos
heard the racket and came racing out of the cabin,
firing his shotgun.

Tod didn't stop running until he got home to
Widow Tweed.

Amos was right behind him. He banged on
Widow Tweed's door.

"That fox was after my chickens!" he shouted
furiously. "If I ever catch him on my property
again, I'll blast him! And next time I won't miss!"

Summer was over.
The cold autumn weather came —
and with it, the hunting season.

Amos loaded his rickety truck with food, blankets,
a tent, and some animal traps. Then he whistled for
Chief and Copper. Off they went on a long hunting trip.

Tod was lonely without Copper. "I wish my friend
would come back," he said to Big Mama.

"He may not *be* your friend when he comes back,"
she said. "He'll be a hunting dog by then. He'll be
trained to hunt foxes, not play with them."

Tod shook his head. "Oh, no. We'll be friends forever."

"Little one," said Big Mama, "forever is a long, long
time. And time has a way of — well, changing things."

All that winter Copper worked side by side with Chief. The old dog taught him to track and hunt and find his way through the silent, snowy woods. Copper grew fond of his teacher, and he learned quickly. By winter's end he was a smart, strong hunting dog.

At the farm, Tod passed the wintry days visiting the animals in the barn and taking long naps in Widow Tweed's warm kitchen. He was growing, too. By springtime he was a sturdy, handsome fox with a fine, bushy tail.

One day in early spring the hunters came home at last.
That night Tod hurried over to visit his old friend.

"You shouldn't be here, Tod," Copper said. "I'm a hunting
dog now, and we can't be friends any more. You'd better
go before Chief wakes up."

Tod's feelings were hurt, but he didn't want Copper to
know. He flicked his tail and tried to look brave. "I'm not
afraid of that old hound," he said loudly.

Chief woke with a start. He lunged at Tod, howling and
barking. Amos rushed out of the cabin, holding his shotgun.

"Run, Tod!" Copper cried. "Run! I'll lead him the wrong
way!"

Tod raced into the night, his heart pounding. The dogs and the hunter were close behind him. Tod ran up a steep hill, then started across a high wooden railroad bridge.

Keeping his promise, Copper led Amos away from the bridge. Tod sighed with relief as he watched them go. But he had forgotten about Chief. Suddenly the fierce old dog was in front of him.

"*Growrr!*" snarled Chief, showing his sharp teeth.

Tod ran back across the bridge. Just then a train came roaring out of the darkness. It sped along the high trestle, heading straight for Tod. He flattened himself between the rails. The train swooshed by, just missing him. But Chief was too big to get out of the way. The train grazed his side, and he tumbled off the bridge.

The old dog landed at the bottom of the ravine. He was badly hurt, and Copper and Amos rushed over to help him.

"It's all that fox's fault!" shouted the hunter.

Copper thought so, too. He looked up at Tod, who was watching from the bridge.

Forgetting about their friendship, Copper growled, "I'll get even with you for this, Tod. Someday, I'll get even!"

Widow Tweed had been out looking for Tod. When she found him he was sad and tired but unhurt. She took him home and locked the door.

Later that night Amos banged on the door. Widow Tweed wouldn't let him in. "I'll get that fox!" Amos bellowed as he stomped away. "I'll get him if it's the last thing I do!"

Widow Tweed knew that Tod would be in danger as long as he stayed on the farm. She had to do something to protect him.

"Tomorrow," she said to Tod, "I'll take you to the game preserve. That's a special place where hunting and trapping aren't allowed. You'll be safe there."

Early next morning they started off in the car. "I'll miss you, Tod," said Widow Tweed sadly. "I'll miss you very much."

At first Tod was lonely and unhappy in the huge game preserve. But soon Big Mama came to visit him. And he began to make friends. He met an old badger and a prickly porcupine. And he met a lovely female fox named Vixey.

"It's not bad here," Tod decided. "I miss Copper and Widow Tweed — but I do like Vixey. And at last I'm safe from Amos Slade."

But the grumpy hunter hadn't forgotten Tod. Chief's leg was still bandaged up, and Amos wanted revenge. Early one morning he whistled for Copper, started his truck, and drove off to the game preserve.

"Hunting isn't allowed there," he mumbled. "But we won't really do any hunting — except to get us a certain no-good little fox!"

Copper growled in agreement.

Amos soon found Tod's tracks in the woods. On a narrow path through the trees, he set some traps and covered them with leaves.

"Now," he whispered to Copper, "we'll let that critter walk right into our hands."

Before long Tod came trotting along with Vixey. When they got to the path, Vixey stopped short.

"What's wrong?" Tod asked.

"Let's go back," Vixey said. "It's too quiet here. All the birds and animals have gone away. This path isn't safe, Tod."

But Tod wouldn't listen. He started off alone. Suddenly —

CLANG! CLANG!

He leaped back just in time. Amos's traps banged shut all around him.

"*Run*, Vixey!" Tod cried.

The frightened foxes raced
through the woods. Amos and
Copper followed close behind them.
Tod and Vixey dove into a burrow,
then darted out the other side. They
scrambled up a rocky hill near a
rushing river. The chase went on
and on.

Copper kept right on the foxes'
trail, leading Amos closer and
closer. Suddenly — *CLANG!* — one
of Amos's own traps clamped shut
on the hunter's leather boot!
Then —

GRROWWL! A grizzly bear came crashing through the bushes. He headed straight for Amos Slade!

The huge bear swiped at Amos, knocking the gun from his hand. With his foot caught in the trap, Amos was helpless. Copper rushed to his side. Growling and snarling, the brave dog charged at the bear.

The bear slapped Copper aside. Copper got up and charged again. Again the huge grizzly flung him to the ground. Now the bear closed in. He reared on his hind legs and raised his powerful paws.

Copper shut his eyes. "I'm done for," he thought.

Suddenly something small and furry flashed
through the air. It landed on the grizzly's head
and hung on tightly.

It was Tod. He had been watching the fight from
a ledge. He hadn't forgotten about the trouble on the
bridge. He knew that Copper blamed him for what
had happened. But Tod didn't care. All that mattered
now was that Copper had been his friend. And his
friend was in danger.

With an angry roar, the bear lunged and whirled,
trying to shake Tod loose. Time and again, Tod
crashed to the ground. Time and again, he got up
and leaped at the bear.

From a high rock, Vixey watched the battle.
Tod looked nearly exhausted. But he kept fighting.

Nearby was the river, where a waterfall rushed and
tumbled onto jagged rocks below. Lying across the
waterfall, almost like a bridge, was an old fallen tree.
　　With a sweep of his paw, the grizzly flung Tod out
onto the tree trunk. Tod's head was spinning. He
gasped for breath and clung to the wobbly tree.

Growling, the bear lumbered out to finish the little fox. But he was too heavy for the old tree trunk. With a loud *CRRRACK!* it split in two.

Down, down went Tod and the bear, over the waterfall and into the rushing, churning water. The huge bear was swept away in the swift current. But where was Tod? Vixey ran to the river's edge to look for him.

"Tod!" she cried. "Where are you?"

At last Tod came up to the surface. He climbed slowly out of the water, scratched and bruised.

Amos had finally managed to pull his foot out of the trap.
As he saw Tod coming out of the river, he reached for his gun.
"At last I've got him," the hunter snarled.
He raised his gun and pointed it at Tod.

Now it was Copper's turn to help his friend.
He came forward and stood between Amos and Tod.

"Get out of the way, Copper," said Amos.

But Copper refused to budge. He looked up at his
master and growled. "Don't you hurt my friend," he
seemed to say. "He was very brave. He saved us both
from the grizzly bear."

The hunter lowered his gun.
He stared at his faithful hound
guarding the fox. For the first
time, Amos understood the deep
friendship between the two animals.
   "Come on, Copper," he said
gruffly. "Come on, boy. Let's go
home."

With Copper sitting beside him, Amos drove his truck down the road and away from the game preserve.

Tod and Vixey watched them from a hill. Copper looked up at Tod as the truck drove off. Tod looked down at Copper. They both knew something important now. They knew that they would always be special friends.

"Very special friends..."
Tod whispered, "forever."